Switched Up!

By Tess Sharpe
Illustrated by Francesco Legramandi
and Grabriella Matta

Random House 🏠 New York

Copyright © 2020 DC Comics.
DC SUPER HERO GIRLS and all related characters and elements
© & ™ DC Comics and Warner Bros. Entertainment Inc.
WB SHIELD: ™ & © WBEI. (s20)

All rights reserved. Published in the United States by Random House Children's Books,
a division of Penguin Random House LLC, 1745 Broadway, New York, NY 10019, and
in Canada by Penguin Random House Canada Limited, Toronto. Random House and
the colophon are registered trademarks of Penguin Random House LLC.

Visit us on the Web!
rhcbooks.com
dcsuperherogirls.com
dckids.com

Library of Congress Cataloging-in-Publication Data is available upon request.
ISBN 978-1-9848-9506-6 (trade) — ISBN 978-1-9848-9507-3 (library binding) —
ISBN 978-1-9848-9508-0 (ebook)

Printed in the United States of America
10 9 8 7 6 5 4 3 2 1

Chapter 1

A Big Copycat
Named Doris Zeul

Kara Danvers was many things: A secret super hero. An aspiring musician. A good friend (she hoped!). A rebel down to her Girl of Steel bones. And, despite being a rebel, a prepared test-taker.

She didn't have the mega–science smarts of her lab partner, Karen Beecher. Karen was a brilliant engineering and science type who had created the battle suit she wore as her secret identity, Bumblebee. Karen had been nice enough to give her a few test quizzes—and Kara had aced them.

So Kara had felt ready to take on any challenge their science teacher threw at them. But rumors that this latest test was the hardest one Mr. Kincaid had ever created were flying around Metropolis High. That made her nervous. Had she studied hard enough?

"We got the lucky spots in the middle!" Karen exclaimed as the two partners entered the lab.

"What's lucky about it?" Kara asked.

"I don't like being up front where everyone can see me," Karen said. "But I can't see the board in the back. So the middle is just right."

"Sounds like a real science, Goldilocks!" Kara teased. "But you're a science *star*, Karen. You should be front and center."

"No thanks!" Karen shook her head. The two girls sat down at their table. "*You* look nervous, Kara."

"I heard the test was hard," Kara confessed. "I hope I get a good grade."

"I brought extra pencils! Who needs one?" Their friend Barbara Gordon, better known as Babs, bounced over to them. Babs was the tech whiz of their friends. She could do anything with computers and gadgets. She could probably ace this science test blindfolded.

"Me, please," Diana Prince said. Babs handed her a pencil. "Oh! These pencils have mighty warrior steeds painted on them!"

"*Unicorns,*" Babs explained.

Diana, an Amazon princess— and exchange student—from the island Themyscira, frowned. She wasn't familiar with all the myths and legends of the World of Man, as she called it.

"These horses have weapons attached to their foreheads. To aid them in battle, yes?" Diana asked.

"Not exactly." Kara smiled—though she could imagine herself in a motorcycle jacket, riding a rock and roll unicorn into battle.

"I'll explain unicorns after the test," Babs told Diana. The Amazon nodded solemnly, as though an unbreakable vow had just been agreed to.

"Maybe we can go see some," she said eagerly.

"Um, maybe!" Babs replied.

"I need a pencil, too, Babs!" Harleen Quinzel waved to Babs, even though she was at the table right next to Kara and Karen's. Doris Zeul sat beside her, frantically reading through their science textbook.

"Oh no," Karen whispered to Kara. "It looks

like Doris forgot the test was today."

When the bell rang, the students hurried to their lab tables. Mr. Kincaid was strict about not talking, no matter what, once a test had started. Kara blew the blond lock of hair that always hung down from her bangs, and gave Karen a confident smile. But inside, she was anything but confident. She felt like Kryptonite butterflies were banging around in her steel stomach until she got past the first two questions.

Later, when she glanced up at the clock to make sure she would have enough time to check her work at the end, Kara noticed that Doris was leaning across her table, staring at Karen's test!

Kara glared at Doris, who just smirked at her. "The nerve!" Kara fumed. "How dare she copy Karen's work!"

Kara nudged Karen underneath the lab table. Karen needed to cover her paper. But Karen was so focused on her own work, she didn't even look up. So Kara glared at Doris some more. Being a rock and roll rebel was all well and good in most instances, but Kara wouldn't stand for cheating.

Stop copying, she mouthed at Doris. She didn't dare say it out loud. Mr. Kincaid's rule about no talking really meant *no talking.*

Doris smiled and mouthed, *I can't hear you.*

Kara felt like her entire body might explode in anger. What a fiend!

Kara knocked her foot lightly against Karen's underneath the table. Karen looked up at her, confused. Kara jerked her chin toward Doris.

Karen sighed and shook her head firmly at Kara. She wanted Kara to drop it. But Kara couldn't drop it. Why should Doris get away with cheating?

But Kara also respected her friend. She knew Karen didn't like being the center of attention. Kara didn't really understand that. She loved attention! Still, she didn't want to do something that would make Karen feel bad.

So Kara turned back to her paper. There were only ten minutes before class was over, and she still had three more questions to answer.

She took a deep breath and focused. She managed to answer them all before looking up again. This time, Doris had taken it too far! She was leaning halfway across the aisle to look at Karen's paper!

"Stop it, Doris!" Kara snapped. Those words came out so loud and so fast that the floor rumbled a little! "Whoops!" Kara slapped her hand over her mouth.

Luckily, things like floor rumbles and mysterious happenings were kind of normal at Metropolis High. Not so luckily, Kara had broken Mr. Kincaid's biggest test rule: no talking!

Karen looked at her with wide, shocked eyes. She couldn't believe Kara would go this far. Breaking the test rule was a big deal.

"Ms. Danvers, what do you think you're doing?" Mr. Kincaid asked.

"Doris is copying Karen's test. She's been doing it this whole time," Kara said. "I can't

stand by while such an—an . . . *injustice* occurs!"

"Hear, hear!" Diana cheered, raising her fist in passionate support.

"Ms. Prince, that is quite enough!" Mr. Kincaid shook his head in disappointment.

"Mr. Kincaid, Kara was just trying to defend me," Karen said, looking terrified at breaking the no-talking rule herself.

"I just don't know what they're talking about, Mr. Kincaid," Doris said, batting her eyes innocently.

"She's lying!" Kara protested.

Harleen, who was sitting next to Doris, looked up from her test with a very annoyed frown. She scribbled something on her paper and then held it up. In addition to her test already being neatly completed, the outer edges of the page were covered in doodles and on the top of the paper she had written in big block letters: Be quiet! I'm doodlin'!

"That's enough," Mr. Kincaid said as Harleen put her test down before he could see her note. "I will deal with the four of you—Ms. Zeul included—after classes today . . . in detention. Disrupting the test like this is not acceptable."

Kara slumped back in her seat, defeated. She knew from fighting villains and evil that justice was hard-won. But now she'd gotten her friends in trouble. She felt horrible . . . and steaming mad at Doris.

The bell rang and the students gathered up their tests to turn in. Doris was one of the first people out the door.

Kara grumbled as she watched her leave.

"Oh, Kara," Karen sighed. "I wish you had just let it go."

"It wasn't fair that she was copying your test," Kara insisted. "You're one of the smartest people in school, *and* you work so hard. Doris shouldn't get to steal that from you!"

13

Karen smiled at her friend. Kara's passion and rebellious spirit were amazing. They also got her in trouble. And now they had gotten *them* in trouble.

"I'm sorry I got you roped into detention," Kara said.

"It's okay," Karen replied. "Detention in the science lab may be a punishment for some . . . like, say, Doris. But I think it will be good practice."

"For what?" Kara asked.

"For when I have a lab that's bigger than the one in my basement!"

Kara grinned. "Only *you* would be excited about detention."

"Let's just get through it together," Karen said. "And no more fights with Doris!"

Kara sighed. This was going to be one long detention session.

Chapter 2

Harleen Quinzel . . .
in the Lab . . .
with a Pumpkin

Babara Gordon was done with her classes for the day. She was going to meet up with her friend Harleen and get some triple-sprinkle donuts at Sweet Justice. But after the ruckus in science class, Babs was worried about her friends.

"I can't believe Mr. Kincaid gave you all detention," Babs said to Diana by their lockers. She was waiting for Harleen to arrive. Harleen was usually late to everything.

"It is a price we must pay in the name of

loudly calling for justice," Diana said solemnly. "It was wrong of Doris to try to copy Karen's test. I do not regret speaking in support."

"What are you two talking about?" Zee Zatara, a magician's assistant and resident fashionista, asked as she strolled up. Zee was carrying a pumpkin tucked under her arm.

"Detention," the two girls chorused.

Zee made a face. "Kara was glaring at Doris all through lunch. If looks could scramble brains, we'd be in trouble!"

"How is Kara going to get through detention with her?" Babs wondered.

"I do not know," Diana said. "But I guess I shall find out. Mr. Kincaid told us to clean the science lab from top to bottom."

"I think I'd better come with you," Zee said. "Together, we can all make sure Kara doesn't melt anyone with her heat vision . . . or worse!"

Babs made sure no one could overhear them. She spotted Harleen skipping down the hall. Her friend had a giant red-and-blue slushie that was slowly melting into purple.

"Hiya, everyone!" Harleen said. "Are you ready for triple-sprinkle donuts?" she asked Babs.

Babs explained to her the change of plans. At first, she was worried Harleen would be upset. But Harleen beamed with delight.

"I *love* detention!" she cackled. "Detention is even better than rainbow sprinkles! And I *love* rainbow sprinkles! Let's go!"

 So together, the girls headed to the science lab to help the rest of their friends clean it up. Karen, Kara, and Doris were already there. Jessica Cruz, one of their good friends, was also there. Jessica was an environmentalist who fought for the earth and its

residents every day. She was also secretly a member of the Green Lantern Corps. Today, she was on a quest to replace the lab soaps with eco-friendly ones. Luckily, Mr. Kincaid was just as passionate about the environment as Jessica, and he had been very supportive of her many environmental campaigns.

Karen and Kara sat at one lab table, scrubbing test tubes covered with green goo. Doris was cleaning that same green goo off another table. It looked like the freshman biology class had spilled a bunch of pond slime everywhere. It certainly smelled like it!

"I have brought friends to help," Diana declared as she swept inside the lab with the gusto of a warrior going into battle. Back on her home island, her mother was Queen of the Amazons. That meant that Diana was royalty. But even royalty had to serve detention!

Doris snorted, like the idea of friends helping was ridiculous.

"What are you doing here, Jess?" Zee asked, sashaying into the lab with her pumpkin.

"First, I'm swapping out the lab soaps," Jessica said. "Then I'm designing a rooftop garden."

"Speaking of gardens . . . ," Karen said. "Zee, why do you have a pumpkin?"

"Ooh, I want to know that, too!" Harleen squealed. "Is it for *smashin'*?"

"And make a bigger mess for us to clean up?" Doris snarled. "I don't think so! You Goody Two-shoes have already ruined my day!"

Harleen pouted and slurped her slushie. Kara glared at Doris, who rolled her eyes and went back to cleaning the lab table.

"The pumpkin is for a magic trick I'm doing with my father," Zee said. Zee's father was a famous magician, and she worked as his assistant. She had been so excited when he loved the pumpkin trick she had dreamed up.

But he wouldn't love it if the orange gourd got smashed!

Zee didn't like the gleam in Harleen's eyes when she looked at the pumpkin, so she put it on the lab cabinet near the fish tank. She smiled as the shark in the tank made a splash at the surface of the water. Then she joined her friends in cleaning up the lab.

"It stinks in here," Doris complained, wiping some of the green goo off her hand. "And it's not just because I have to be around a bunch of goody-goodies."

"I'll open the windows!" Harleen dropped her broom to the ground. It almost crashed into a set of clean test tubes. She flung the windows open, breathing in the fresh air. Then she nearly knocked over the robot project Babs kept in the science lab.

"Careful!" Babs called out. She hurried over, snatching her robot out of the way. "That's for my science fair project."

"Sorry!" Harleen said cheerfully. She took a long sip of her slushie. "I'll watch where I'm going."

"Why don't you feed the shark?" Kara suggested to Harleen. "Mr. Kincaid said we needed to feed her, too."

Harleen liked the sound of that. Mr. Kincaid kept the shark's tank covered during their science class. The shark slept until the afternoon. Their class was in the morning, so she never got a good look at the toothy gal. Harleen wished she could sleep in. If only she could live the life of a shark. She'd swim around and snap her teeth at anyone who messed with her. And she'd never have to go to school—she'd just have schools of fish to eat!

Harleen bent down to look the shark in the

24

eye. When the small shark saw Harleen, it snarled. It had so many teeth! She grinned, baring her own teeth back at the shark. The creature swam toward Harleen, tapping its snout against the glass. Harleen giggled and did the same.

"She likes you," Diana said. She held out a jar of shark food. It was a brighter purple than Harleen's slushie. Harleen wondered if the food should be that color. Wasn't fish food brown and flaky and kind of stinky?

"The shark comes from the waters surrounding my homeland," Diana said. "I brought her back with me the last time I visited

home—to show Mr. Kincaid. He wrote a paper about her! This Themysciran water plant is her favorite treat."

Diana handed Harleen the jar. She plucked out a piece of purple plant and dropped it into the tank. The shark gobbled it up in seconds.

"This is my kind of detention," Harleen said. She gave the shark another treat. It chomped and snapped. The purple leaf stuck between the shark's teeth in the same way that spinach sometimes got stuck in Harleen's. Poor shark! She couldn't exactly offer it a toothpick or some floss. A few more treats and Harleen's job was all done. She knew she should help the others clean—that would be the *good* thing to do. But Harleen wasn't exactly good at *being* good.

Harleen was secretly the villainous Harley Quinn, which meant she was fearless and bad to the bone. But Harleen Quinzel knew not to cause too much trouble when there was

a cranky science teacher waiting to check on the lab. A smart villain was one who knew how to lie low at the right time. "But a true villain also doesn't mop floors," she thought. That was what minions were for. "Rats!" She had none—minions or rats!

Harleen turned away from the shark and spotted Karen, who was trying to put a rack of clean test tubes on the top shelf of the lab cabinet. But even on her tiptoes, Karen couldn't reach. Harleen to the rescue! She zipped over to the cabinet.

"I can help!" she chirped.

Karen jumped. The test tubes rattled in her hands. "Oh! Harleen! You scared me!"

"Let me take these." Harleen whisked the test tubes out of Karen's hands. She wasn't tall enough to reach the top shelf, either. But no worries—she knew a way. She'd just climb it.

Harleen grabbed the top shelf of the cabinet and swung her legs up. The shelves

rattled. The bottles on the shelves slid. Karen, who was standing below, gasped, "Eep!"

The cabinet began to fall forward. Harleen shrieked. She was going to fall on Karen! Then the cabinet would squash them both flatter than a couple of pancakes!

Chapter 3

This Is Another Fine Mess You've Gotten Us Into!

Kara dashed forward as the science cabinet began to fall. Harleen had scrambled up it like a squirrel before Kara could shout to stop her! Bottles and jugs of chemicals tipped off the shelves and crashed onto the ground in front of them. A puddle of pink foam bubbled up from the accidental concoction and spread across Karen's shoes. *Yikes!*

Luckily, Kara was able to push the cabinet back up before it crashed onto Karen's head. Super-strength and super-speed came in handy in just about any situation.

Harleen let go of the shelf as soon as Kara steadied the cabinet. She tumbled out of the way with acrobatic grace as Zee's pumpkin crashed down to the floor. *Splat!* It smashed into hundreds of pieces, splattering the pink foam. Kara winced as a piece of pumpkin hit her in the face. Karen was covered with pumpkin and bubbling pink foam.

"My slushie!" Harleen wailed, having already forgotten the trouble she had caused. "It's ruined!"

"You almost squished us!" Karen protested angrily. "And you're worried about a slushie?!"

"It's okay," Kara said quietly. "Harleen was just trying to help." She took a deep breath. She felt funny. Wobbly. In fact, that was what her lip was doing. Wobbling, like she was about to cry. This day had been terrible! First she got detention for standing up for her friend. Now she was covered in slimy pumpkin and pink foam . . . and . . . and . . .

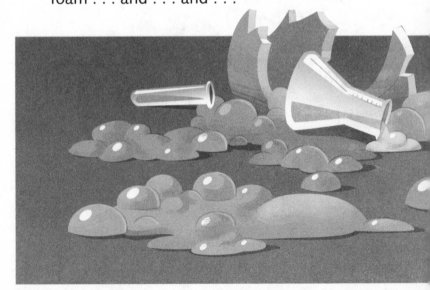

Kara gave her head a quick shake. Wait a second. Why was she feeling so upset? She should be mad, like Karen, not sad!

The door to the science lab burst open. Mr. Kincaid stood there, staring at the giant mess. Everyone froze guiltily in place.

Kara and Karen were dripping with gunk. Diana was shielding the shark tank from falling pumpkin bits, while Jessica crouched near the window with her research books.

Harleen was still clutching her ruined slushie and pouting. As usual, Doris just glared at everyone. Zee stared at the ruined pumpkin—and then up at their teacher. And Babs looked like she was trying to fade into the wall as she realized what a fine mess they'd all gotten themselves into. They were in *so* much trouble now.

"What in the world is going on here?" Mr. Kincaid asked.

"It was an accident!" Karen said.

"We can explain," Kara said at the same time.

"This is the *biggest* mess I've ever seen," Mr. Kincaid said. *"And I teach freshman biology!"*

"Thank you?" Babs suggested.

"He did not mean it as a compliment," Diana whispered loudly.

The girls grouped together, away from the mess. Having your teacher mad at you was no fun. Especially when you kind of deserved it. He had told them to clean up the lab. But now it was much, much worse.

"We are in so much trouble," Jessica groaned.

"You'd need superpowers to clean this place up," their teacher said, and shook his head, bewildered. "I am disappointed in you girls. I thought that one day of detention would be enough to teach you the power of getting along. But it looks like you'll need more. A whole week's worth."

The girls gasped. An entire week of detention?

Doris growled under her breath in the corner. This was so unfair. She had nothing to do with the mess the goody-goodies had just caused. She hadn't even brought the pumpkin into the lab. More detention meant she was going to miss her after-school workout for a whole week. She had been practicing how to throw the shot put, an ancient sport of strength that she wanted to master. Being strong and powerful was what she did best.

Doris smiled at the thought of her secret identity, Giganta. She loved putting one over on an entire city of adults! Almost as much as she loved roaming through Metropolis and causing trouble. Though those pesky super hero girls always seemed to show up at the exact right time to ruin her plans.

Now she'd have no time to train. Not with all this detention! Doris glared at Kara. This was all her fault. If she'd just kept quiet about the test, Doris would be hurling heavy stuff across the school's track field to her heart's content. But no, Kara had to stick her nose into Doris's business.

Mr. Kincaid sent Kara and Karen to go clean up. They were dripping pumpkin bits and pink foam all over the floor. There was even pumpkin in Karen's sneakers! It squished with each step as she marched purposefully toward the locker room.

The other girls headed to the janitor's closet. They were going to need a much bigger mop to get this mess cleaned up!

Chapter 4

Magic Squash and a Superpowers Switcheroo!

After cleaning the pink foam and pumpkin off themselves in the locker room, Kara and Karen changed into their gym clothes.

"I can't believe I have to wear this home," Kara said. She tugged at the neck of her T-shirt. "Everyone will stare at me!"

Karen rolled her eyes. "You really need to chill out," she said. Her jaw dropped. "I don't know why I just said that!"

Kara's stomach sank. It was like before, when she'd gotten sad instead of mad. *Karen* was the one who worried about people staring.

Kara was usually the one who told *her* to chill out!

The door to the locker room banged open. Zee came running toward them as fast as her fashionable shoes could carry her.

"Zee, you seem upset," Kara said.

The magician's assistant was out of breath. She must have run all the way from the janitor's closet. "Are you two feeling anything other than sticky?"

The two girls stared at her. Karen did not like the guilty look on Zee's face.

"Because the pumpkin might have been just a *little* bit magic," Zee explained.

"What kind of magic?" Kara asked in alarm.

"Oh, great—a magic pumpkin." Karen rolled her eyes. "Does this make you our fairy godmother?"

Zee's eyes widened. Karen was never snarky like that! "The spell was technically *inside* the pumpkin. *But* the pieces mixed with the chemicals in the lab cabinet. I think we're dealing with a mix of magic, squash, *and* science!"

"What does that mean?" Kara asked. She twisted her hands worriedly.

"The pumpkin had a switching spell cast on it," Zee explained. "Pumpkins are very good for spells. That's why they're in all the fairy tales. But my spell was just supposed to switch a rabbit into a dove. I don't know what it'll do to humans."

"Oh no!" Kara said, her lip started trembling again. "I'm not human. What's it going to do to *me*?"

Zee frowned. Kara was acting worried. And Karen was cracking jokes that sounded like *Kara*. Was it possible that her spell had switched their personalities?

Zee had no idea what that weird foam was other than a nice shade of pink. The chemical mix could have changed the spell in all sorts of ways.

"Kara, can you yank this locker door off?" Zee asked. She needed to make sure that it was only her friends' personalities that were switched.

"And damage school property?" Kara asked. She was scandalized that Zee would even think she'd do such a thing. But wait . . . she had totally done that before. Why was she feeling so worried about it now?

"I'll magic it back," Zee promised.

Kara yanked at the door with one hand. Normally, her super-strength would make the job easy. But the door wouldn't budge. She

pulled with both hands . . . and still nothing! Tucking her tongue between her teeth, Kara really put her back—and two feet—into it. Nada!

"I don't understand," she told Zee.

"I think that the spell might have switched your personalities . . . *and* your powers," Zee said.

"What?!" Kara and Karen shrieked together.

"I can't have Kara's powers!" Karen said. "She's super-strong and fast and all

sorts of things that come with super, *super* responsibilities! I haven't prepared! I need to study or take a class or something!"

"Sorry, I don't think there's any Kryptonian 101 at Metropolis High," Kara said gloomily. "Is this why my face keeps getting so hot?" She held her hands against her red cheeks. "Am I blushing?!"

Zee felt terrible that her magic pumpkin had helped cause this chaos. She had to find a way to fix it. First, she needed to make sure her theory was correct—that Karen had Kara's powers as well as her rock and roll personality.

"Karen, can you try to pull the locker door off the hinges?"

Karen rolled her eyes at Zee but did as her friend asked. She gave the door what she thought was a light yank. The entire row of lockers came crashing down!

"I guess that answers our question," Zee said. The magician waved her hands and said,

"Pu dna ta me." Creaking and rattling, the lockers rose back into place.

"Let me just try something," Kara said. She could still fly, right? Zee's spell couldn't have taken all of her powers . . . could it? She jumped into the air. But instead of soaring off, she hovered awkwardly for a few moments and dropped back down.

Kara's face burned with frustration as she realized that Zee and Karen were staring at her. This was so embarrassing! She loved to fly. Not being able to do so felt terrible. Almost as terrible as getting stared at. Her lip trembled again. "Stop that!" she thought.

"You try," Kara told Karen.

"I don't know how without my Bumblebee suit," Karen said. But she jumped up at Kara's encouragement . . . and floated off the ground. She was used to flying in her suit. She loved her suit and what she had designed it to do—*and* how it could protect her. But this kind of flying was different. She could feel the air on her face. She wondered if Kara got bugs in her teeth when she flew across Metropolis. "That would be gross!" she thought.

Without thinking, Karen lifted her arms and shot straight up. In fact, she flew up so fast that Kara had to grab her leg to keep her from crashing right through the ceiling.

"Careful!" Kara and Zee pulled Karen down to the ground.

"Whew. Thanks. That's way more liftoff than my suit has," Karen said. "I'm not sure I like it!"

"Zee, how do we fix this?" Kara asked.

"I'll figure it out," Zee said, biting her lip. "I swear by all the tricks up my sleeve. But I need to do some research first. And you two need to act normal tomorrow at school."

"Like that's possible," Karen muttered grumpily. She gasped and pressed her hand against her mouth. Then she winced.

Super-strength was no joke. "This is the worst!" she wailed. "I have *attitude*! My parents will kill me if I come home with attitude. I'll be grounded for life."

"How do you think *I* feel?" Kara asked glumly. "I was going to go to a concert at the Lazarus Pit tonight. But now I feel this strange feeling in my stomach. Like . . . I shouldn't break curfew?"

"That's guilt," Karen told her. "Because you *shouldn't* break curfew! Or . . . maybe you should. A concert sounds fun. Wait. No!

I don't go to loud concerts. I don't know! I'm confused!"

"Both of you should go home," Zee said. "And try to act as much like you—the *real yous*—as possible."

"You better figure out how to fix this, Zee," Karen demanded. Then she made a face. "I'm sorry. I shouldn't have said that."

Zee reached out and gave her friend a hug. Karen hugged her back. And then Kara joined in. Sometimes you just needed a hug. This was one of those times. Instantly, all three girls felt better. Together with the rest of their friends, they would find a way to fix this. Even if Zee had to . . . *shudder* . . . do science to solve the power switcheroo.

Chapter 5

It's All Fun and Games Until Someone Breaks the Floor

Acting normal when you felt the exact opposite was like putting on a sweater three sizes too small. When Karen arrived at school the next morning, she had a scowl on her face. She could hear *everything*. Her vision was sharper. With every step she took, she felt a mix of worried and excited, thinking she'd just lift off into the air. Or she might stomp too hard on the ground and break something. Who knew what could happen? She'd woken up this morning floating three feet above her bed instead of in it!

"How do you handle all this?" she asked Kara as they walked the crowded halls of Metropolis High. Every few seconds, she would twitch, whipping her head around to look down the hall. Super-hearing was so annoying! She didn't want to overhear people's conversations! She felt super-nosy, not superpowered! But now she couldn't avoid it. "Is there a way to turn the super-hearing off?"

Kara shot her a sympathetic look. "You just get used to it," she confessed. "I could barely sleep last night. Everything was too quiet!"

"You think that's bad? I woke up this morning hovering above the bed!"

Kara reddened. "Sorry. I should've warned you that sleep-flying might happen. It's like sleepwalking, except you know . . . *not.*"

"I'm just glad my mom didn't come into my room to wake me up. I'm not going to fly out the window or something, am I?"

Karen looked alarmed at the thought.

Kara shook her head. "It's just a hovering thing. No flying out the window involved. Just set your alarm early so your mom doesn't catch you."

Karen reached for the doorknob of the door to their first class, not thinking as she yanked it hard. Normally, the door was heavy and hard to pull open. But now, with her borrowed girl-of-steel strength, the knob came right off in her hand!

"Oh no!" Kara said. "I hate damaging school property!"

"No, *I* hate it," Karen hissed. "Or I used to."

The two girls scrambled to hide the doorknob behind their backs as a group of teachers walked by talking about Hal Jordan's latest victory on the basketball court. Hal was known to be a little full of himself, and he liked to be the star of anything athletic. So it was no wonder that he was the school's star basketball player.

Luckily, they were so busy talking about Hal's perfectly executed three-pointer that no one noticed the damaged door. As soon as the teachers passed, the girls spun around and tried to fix the door before their English teacher arrived.

"You're going to need to use your heat vision to fuse it," Kara whispered, looking over her shoulder to make sure no one was around.

"I don't know how," Karen protested.

Kara tried to think of a good way to describe what it felt like to melt things with your eyes. Mostly, it felt *awesome*. Because it *was* awesome. It was one of her most awesome powers, if you asked her. She could melt metal *and* toast marshmallows for s'mores.

"Just look at the doorknob and think . . . hot things," Kara said.

Karen narrowed her eyes. Her mouth twisted in concentration. Her eyes narrowed more. And then, *zzzap!* Her eyes sparked up just enough to melt the doorknob back on the door.

"I did it!"

Before the girls could rejoice, their English teacher arrived. She seemed a little confused that the doorknob was so warm as she led them into class. Soon, the rest of their friends joined them.

"How's the power switcheroo going?" Zee asked from her desk behind Karen's.

"My mom almost caught me sleep-flying!" Karen whispered back. "Please tell me you've found a way to fix this!"

"Jessica and I are on it," Zee said. "She knows plants, so I need her expertise when it comes to the squash side of our problem."

55

Karen felt a little better knowing Jessica and Zee were working hard to solve the problem. If she talked back to her mom like she had wanted to at dinner or got caught floating, she was going to be in so much trouble.

The girls had gym class next. Normally, this was one of Kara's favorite classes. She loved showing her strength and agility, but now she found herself feeling unsure and kind of small as everyone lined up in teams for volleyball.

Kara wasn't used to feeling unsure about *anything*. Even when she didn't have a plan—which was most of the time—she was always confident in the moves she made up on the spot. Being indestructible was a real confidence booster.

As the teams volleyed the ball back and forth across the net, Kara missed the ball twice. Then she got hit in the face because she hadn't dodged fast enough! Her cheeks burned in embarrassment. Being human was

Tough with a capital T.

In front of her, Karen was right up at the volleyball net with Diana. Diana's Amazon warrior training served her well in gym class. She leaped and ran and dived for the volleyball like the fate of a battle depended on it. But Karen was struggling as much as Kara was—for different reasons. She was scared that if she hit the volleyball too hard, she would make it explode or something! Kara's super-strength wasn't easy to control. So when the ball came flying toward Karen, she tapped it with the tips of her fingers. The ball flew into the net.

"Karen! That was an easy one," Harleen complained.

"Sorry," Karen called behind her. "I think my hands are sweaty." She wiped them on her gym shirt.

She needed to hit the ball with more force—but how much? The scientist in her wanted to run all sorts of tests to see what she could and couldn't do. Kara's powers broke the laws of physics, which meant that *Karen* could break those laws. And with Kara's feisty personality swirling inside her, the thought of breaking stuff seemed *great.*

Karen was so distracted thinking about how cool it would be to travel faster than

the speed of light that she didn't realize that she had started bouncing the ball. The more she thought, the harder she bounced the ball. Super-speed! Heat vision! Super-breath! Super-streng—

Pow! Slap! Crack!

The entire gym class watched in shock as the volleyball smashed into the floor and *broke* it!

Karen snatched her hands behind her back, trying to look innocent as Kara raced up to her and Diana looked at them both in concern.

"Mrs. Lake, we can explain," Kara said, trying to think of a plausible explanation to give their gym teacher. But when the teacher looked at her sternly, she found she had no words. Her cheeks just turned bright red, and she began to fall into a big bowl of word soup! "You see . . . the basketball team . . . they were playing in the gym yesterday. They must've weakened the floor. That's why the volleyball broke it."

Mrs. Lake frowned and crossed her arms. She began to tap her foot. Kara was not selling the explanation. Probably because *Karen* was bad at lying. Like, the worst.

But then, to Kara and Karen's relief, Hal bounced over from the other side of the gym. "You know," he said. "I think I do remember the floor making some funny sounds when we were practicing yesterday. I bet my dunking and dribbling broke the floor, just like Kara said."

"Hmm, I guess I'll take your word for it," Mrs. Lake said. Hal's confidence was hard to resist. And he certainly seemed to believe it. "But I don't want you playing on a cracked floor, so let's go outside and run laps instead."

Everyone but Diana groaned.

"Close call," Karen whispered.

"Zee can't figure out how to switch us back fast enough," Kara muttered. "She better do it before we accidentally break the entire school."

"You mean before *I* break the entire school," Karen grumbled.

"Hey, we're in this together," Kara promised, showing a glimmer of her usual self. "We'll figure it out."

Karen wasn't so sure. But she hoped Kara was right.

Chapter 6

Hay Is for Horses
(and Mazes and Goats)

After gym class, Diana caught up with Karen at their lockers. Diana wore a worried expression. "Karen, what happened in gym class today? It was almost as if you came to school this morning with the strength of the Amazons!"

"More like the strength of Kara," Karen said. She explained to Diana about the switcheroo and how Zee and Jessica were doing magic, science, and squash research to undo it.

"I will aid Zee and Jessica in this noble quest!" Diana said, placing her hand over her heart in a solemn vow. "We will not rest until you have returned to your wonderful selves."

"I would love your help, Diana," Zee said as she strolled up to their lockers with a dejected-looking Kara in tow. "I think this is an all-hands-on-deck situation. We should meet to do more research."

"I'm good at research," Karen said. "Or . . . I was. But Kara's great at studying, too."

"Not as great as you," Kara pointed out. "I would love to make a plan, but the Kents are coming today. I promised I'd help them unload the hay they're delivering to PawPaw's

Pumpkin Patch. He's building a hay-bale maze for his goats."

"Not for his pumpkin-patch guests?" Zee asked, looking confused.

"PawPaw loves everyone who comes to the pumpkin patch," Kara said. "But he loves his goats more than *anything*. And they liked the maze we made them last year . . . well, until they ate it. But I think that's part of the fun for them."

Karen snickered at the idea of goats solving a maze and then eating it. "Or maybe they solved the maze *by* eating it," she thought. This she had to see!

"You look concerned, Kara Danvers," Diana said. "Tell me what troubles your spirit so I may share your burdens and help you defeat them."

Kara *hated* this blushing thing. She *was* concerned like Diana said. One of the reasons the Kents had asked for her help unloading the hay was because she was super-strong, but now she wasn't anymore. Karen was.

If the Kents noticed that she didn't have her powers, they might think some nefarious villain had given her a Kryptonite smoothie or something. And if she told them the truth, that it had happened at Metropolis High, they might want her to come back to the farm. Or worse, call in the big guy: her cousin. As much as Kara loved the Kents and the farm, she also loved her friends and her classes at Metropolis High. She needed to be careful and watch what she did and said—which was going to be really hard, because she wanted to be honest *all* the

time now. She also wanted to clean her locker as much as she'd cleaned her room. She couldn't stand messiness all of a sudden!

Kara explained to her friends how she needed to help the Kents and how she was worried that they might notice she didn't have her powers.

"This," Diana declared boldly, "is truly a kerfuffle."

"Diana, where did you learn that word?" Zee giggled.

"Harleen taught it to me! I like the word very much. She said I should name the shark in the science lab Kerfuffle."

"What does it mean?" Kara asked. It certainly sounded like the kind of word Harleen would like.

"It means we are in a bit of a mess."

"I guess we are," Zee said. "A kerfuffle indeed. I should've left that pumpkin in my locker. Then you two wouldn't be sleep-flying or worrying about how to pretend to be super-strong when you aren't."

"It's okay, Zee," Kara said. "Who could guess something like this would happen?"

"Why doesn't Karen go with you to make the hay maze?" Zee suggested. "The rest of us will continue to research how to switch you back."

"That sounds like a good plan," Karen said. "What do you say, Kara?"

Kara knew teamwork was important, but it was hard to admit that she was going to need help throwing something as light as a *hay bale*. But she put a determined smile on her face anyway. "Let's go for a hayride."

Chapter 7

Squash—Two Ways . . . and Both Equally Messy!

PawPaw's Pumpkin Patch was at the edge of Metropolis. The hay bales the Kents delivered was stacked high in their truck. At first, Kara were worried they'd notice that Karen was helping her lift the bales, but soon she realized she was in the clear. Everyone just thought she was trying to maintain her secret identity. *Phew!* She hated the idea of worrying the Kents—or anyone.

Transporting the hay to the meadow where PawPaw was building his goat maze was sweaty and sneezy work. By the time Kara and Karen were done unloading the hay and building the entrance to the maze, they smelled like a barn. It made Kara think of the Kents' farm and throwing secret rock concerts in the barn. It took a lot of skill to pull off a secret rock concert, but she'd managed before. More than once.

"Are you sure you girls don't want a ride into the city?" Mr. Kent asked as he prepared to head back to the farm.

"We're going to take the bus, Mr. Kent," Karen explained. "Our friend Jess got us all passes. She's big on being eco-friendly."

"If we don't take care of the earth, she won't take care of us," Mrs. Kent said with a smile. "Don't forget to call me next week about your visit to the farm, Kara."

Kara waved as they drove away in the hay truck.

"That wasn't as hard as I thought," Karen commented.

"You didn't even throw a hay bale across the meadow, except for that one time," Kara agreed. The girls began walking to the bus stop, when Karen stopped in her tracks.

"What is it?" Kara asked.

Karen tapped her ear. "Don't you hear that?"

"What?" she replied, frustrated. She missed her super-hearing so much!

"Someone's screaming at the pumpkin patch. But not in a happy *I found the perfect pumpkin* kind of way."

Kara and Karen exchanged a nervous look.

72

The super hero girls were needed, but could they pull off a mission with their powers switched? They had no choice: where villains were, the super hero girls would appear, to deal out justice and spread good wherever they could.

Kara and Karen dashed into the cornfield to transform. They quickly sent a text to their special super hero girls–text chain to alert the others that they needed help. But PawPaw's Pumpkin Patch was on the very outskirts of Metropolis. It would take the other super heroes a while to get there. Which meant that it was up to Kara and Karen to face whatever was interrupting the fun.

"How is this going to work?" Kara asked. Her heart was hammering inside her chest like a woodpecker's beak against an old oak tree.

"Luckily, I couldn't sleep much the other night because of my new super-hearing," Karen explained. She pulled out her Bumblebee suit. "I made a few changes to my suit so that you can wear it. My suit specifically works for me, so I'm not totally sure how it's going to react to your Kryptonian physiology."

"What are you going to wear?" Kara asked as she pulled the Bumblebee suit on. She could hear the mechanical *buzz* around her as she snapped the helmet on.

"I made *this* for myself." Karen pulled on the suit she'd made. It looked like Supergirl's, but instead of the red and blue that Kara sported, Karen wore a yellow-and-black-bee version.

"Let's go!"

The girls pushed away from the ground. Karen's takeoff was a lot smoother than Kara's. Kara expected to soar up and over the patch of trees in the distance like usual. But the Bumblebee suit buzzed as she rose shakily off the ground. As Supergirl, flying was as easy as walking, but the tech suit required more focused concentration and balance. Flying with

wings was a lot harder than just being able to fly! Hovering ten feet in the air, she pushed forward with her arms like she would as Supergirl and flipped all the way over. She cried out.

"Kara!" Karen circled around her slowly, looking worried.

"Almost got it," Kara promised as she tilted to one side, then the other, trying to get a feel for the wings as Karen hovered in front of her.

She shot forward a little too fast, almost hitting Karen, who squeaked and darted up and out of the way. But as Kara flew toward Karen, the suit's wings flapping so fast they were a blur, she began to understand: Karen and the suit were partners, and now Kara and the suit had to be partners, too. "I'm ready!"

The girls flew to the pumpkin patch—the problem becoming clear instantly.

"It's Giganta!" Kara gasped as they watched the notorious villain stomp through PawPaw's Pumpkin Patch without a care in the world for the squash she was squashing!

"And Harley Quinn is with her!" Karen pointed down to where Harley was waltzing with one of PawPaw's scarecrows, a slushie in one hand. More of the scarecrow's stuffing was coming out with every dramatic twirl she made.

Giganta loved to be large and in charge. But she didn't feel very in charge when she had to

76

spend an entire week in detention. Especially for something she hadn't done. When Mr. Kincaid had said that those Goody Two-shoes Karen and Kara had made the biggest mess he had ever seen, Giganta knew she had something to prove. That mess had been one exploded pumpkin. One! She'd show *everyone* what a mess really was! She had her reputation to protect.

So Giganta had asked Harley Quinn to give her a hand. She wanted only the biggest, wartiest pumpkins, and she'd need time to find them in the pumpkin patch. That meant she needed a partner. Luckily, Harley was up for anything, especially if it involved madcap villainy *and* PawPaw's lovable goats.

Giganta lifted one of the smaller pumpkins out of Harley's wheelbarrow and threw it like a shot-putter. Tossing pumpkins was a great workout! She could feel the burn in her beautifully bulging biceps. She threw another, laughing as it crashed into the goat pen and the goats scrambled out to eat the squash. All around her, people ran for cover, knowing that any minute, they could be next: sticky, squashy, and nibbled by goats!

Giganta took a deep breath. "Ahhhh . . . it feels so good to be so bad!" she said. Destruction! Chaos! Goats on the loose! This truly was the life. And the best part? No pesky super hero girls to stop her!

Just then, something whizzed by the villain's ear. Two somethings.

"Put down the pumpkin, Giganta!"

Two figures hovered in front of her, but Giganta didn't recognize them. One of them was in a high-tech battle suit. There was something different about the bug-girl that Giganta couldn't quite put her big finger on. The other Goody Two-shoes was dressed like Supergirl, but the colors were all wrong! Giganta was confused, but she didn't want to

show that kind of weakness in battle, so she sneered, "Yellow really isn't a good color for either of you."

"Jeepers!" Harley squeaked below as she cartwheeled up to her partner. "Who are you two?"

Kara and Karen exchanged a confused glance.

"Err, we're . . . um," Kara could feel her face getting hot. She wobbled a little in the air. Oh no! Now was not the time to get nervous!

"We're Bumblegirl and Superbee!" Karen said, thinking quickly. "Stop this reign of terror immediately!"

"Or what?" Harley asked, tilting her head curiously. She took a long drink of her slushie.

"Or we'll stop you!" Kara said.

Giganta laughed as she hefted a pumpkin and threw it at the new super heroes.

Chapter 8

New Heroes,
Same Problems

Karen dodged the pumpkin Giganta had just lobbed, spinning away in a tight circle. But she overestimated her speed. She spun all the way across the pumpkin patch and into a tree. A branch above her shook as she crashed into the trunk, and a bird's nest fell on her head.

Karen had to get back to Kara. She was all on her own dealing with two villains! Kara was probably having as much trouble adjusting to the Bumblebee suit as Karen was having adjusting

to Kara's superpowers! She made sure the eggs were safe and carefully put the bird's nest back on the branch it had fallen from. Then she jumped into the air and flew back to the pumpkin patch as fast as she dared.

Kara looked over her shoulder, wishing that Karen would return. She triggered the controls on the suit, shrinking into her tiny bee form. As she shrank and everything got bigger, Kara's head spun. She took a deep breath and shook her head back and forth to clear it. Seeing the world so large was an amazing shift in perspective.

Giganta squeaked in surprise as Kara dived for her head, tugging at one of her curls.

The villain swatted. Kara dived away from Giganta's hand, but she wasn't fast enough. *Bam!* She hit the ground hard, and the unfamiliar battle suit fritzed and sparked, popping her back to her regular size. Kara scrambled away from Giganta's stomping feet, but that brought her right into the path of Harley Quinn!

Harley uncapped her slushie and held it over Kara's head. She smiled as she tipped the cup.

"I think the goats will love a little Superbee slushie treat! Their sandpaper tongues will tickle something awful! You'll giggle yourself purple!" Harley laughed as the goats bleated behind her, eager for a taste of slushie.

"How dare the goats betray me like this!" Kara thought. She had built them their hay-bale maze.

Kara threw her hands up. It was going to take forever to clean the suit after it got slushie and goat spit all over it!

"Watch it," Giganta roared, whirling around and pointing at Harley. "The little bee's mine!" She bent down, her hand lowering to close around Kara.

"Not on your life!" shouted a voice.

Karen burst through the clouds. She shot through the air in a blur, hurtling toward the ground at a speed that made her eyes water. She had found out the hard way: Kara *did* get bugs in her teeth when flying really fast. *So gross!* Karen grabbed Kara around the waist and lifted off before the villain could catch either of them.

"Come back here!" Giganta roared in anger.

"No fair! I just wanted to give the goats a sugary, buggy treat!" Harley wailed.

"You could have just given them the slushie," Kara shouted as she and Karen flew through the air.

Harley scampered off, patting one of the goats on the head as she left. Giganta was close on her heels, the wheelbarrow full of pumpkins tucked underneath her massive arm.

Karen set Kara on the ground. Electricity crackled over the damaged Bumblebee suit. It would take some tinkering in the lab to get it back into working order.

All around them, people peeked out from their hiding places.

"Friends! Warrior sisters! We have arrived!" Diana came running across the meadow disguised as Wonder Woman. She was closely followed by Babs, who was in her purple Batgirl uniform, and Zee, whose magic wand was out and at the ready. Jessica was close

behind, her Green Lantern power ring glowing on her finger.

"Where are our foes?" Batgirl demanded. "Let me at 'em!"

"It was Giganta and Harley Quinn," Kara said. "But they took off after Karen saved me from Harley's slushie."

"What was their purpose here?" Wonder Woman asked, staring across the now-squashed pumpkin field.

"Pumpkin stealing," Karen said. "We don't know why."

Before the super hero girls could continue discussing what Giganta and Harley Quinn were up to, the owner of the pumpkin patch came hurrying up to them.

"Super hero girls, I can't even begin to thank you," PawPaw told them. "You kept us all safe and saved my pumpkin patch."

"That is our sworn duty," Wonder Woman told him. "We are happy to help. But your thanks should rightfully go to my two friends here." She gestured valiantly at Karen and Kara.

"Bumblegirl really deserves all the credit," Kara said. "I would've been just as squashed without her."

Karen's stomach flipped at the compliment. "You would've figured something out," she said.

"Let me give you pumpkins as a thank-you!" PawPaw said, giving each of the heroes their choice of pumpkins. The villains might have gotten away, but Kara and Karen had foiled their plans, avoided getting tickled by the goats, and gotten some free pumpkins. So all in all, this was not bad for a day of super hero work!

Chapter 9

Pumpkin Spice and Everything Nice

Carving pumpkins was sticky, tricky work. Babs stuck her tongue between her teeth as she tried to get the perfect bat symbol carved into her pumpkin.

"Look!" Diana declared, placing her pumpkin on her head. Diana had carved her pumpkin into a mighty battle helmet. Jessica

had explained to Diana the tradition of carving faces or other designs into the pumpkins, but the Amazon princess had wanted to march to the beat of her own drum.

"Errr . . . it looks very fearsome, Diana," Karen said, putting the finishing touches on the bumblebee she had carved into her pumpkin. The stripes weren't as tidy as she would've liked, but it still looked good.

"Don't forget to save all the pumpkin seeds for me," Jessica reminded her friends. She had carved a beautiful sun on her pumpkin.

"Are we going to eat them?" Kara asked.

"I am definitely going to plant some next year," Jessica declared. "Then we can carve pumpkins that we grew ourselves!"

"I could always use a supply of pumpkins," Zee said. She had carved a traditional smiling jack o' lantern face into her pumpkin, but she had added a magician's top hat and wand to give it some flair.

"I think you should probably stay away from mixing pumpkins and magic for a while," Babs pointed out.

"It's the science that messed it all up," Zee insisted.

"Does that mean you've figured out a way to switch us back?" Kara asked eagerly.

"We have some hypotheses," Jessica said. "Soon we'll know all the elements that were in the pink foam. We already know what went into Zee's spell. It's the pink foam that's the mystery."

"But once we know what's in it, we can create an antidote," Karen said, sighing in relief.

"That's the idea," Babs said. "I wonder what was in that pink foam."

"It could've just been lab soap," Kara said.

Zee shook her head. "With the way it reacted? It was something different. Maybe just a strange concoction from the random chemicals that got mixed. Too bad we cleaned it up before realizing we were going to need a sample."

"Maybe it's alien pond slime!" Babs giggled.

"Bigfoot tears," Jessica said, joining in the fun.

"Shark boogers!" Karen suggested.

"Ewww!" Babs laughed. "Sharks don't have boogers."

"What happens when they sneeze, then?" Karen asked.

Diana tapped her pumpkin helmet, thinking. "By great Poseidon, I do not know," she confessed. "My mother would know. She is wise in the ways of battle, leadership, and marine life."

"All *I* know is that I'll be glad when we're switched back," Karen said.

"The longer we stay like this, the weirder it gets," Kara agreed. "I miss rocking out."

"I never want to sleep-fly again!" Karen said. "And my parents are so mad about

how messy my room is now. I was never messy before. My workshop looks like it exploded. And the other night, I snuck out late and went moshing at the Lazarus Pit. Moshing! *Me!* And I loved it!"

"What about me?" Kara asked over her pumpkin. "I want to color-code my closet and keep everything neat. I almost volunteered to clean test tubes after chemistry class *for fun*! The thing that I was doing in detention!"

"Cleanliness is very important in the lab!" Karen, Jessica, and Babs said in unison.

Kara shook her head. "No one should think cleaning out a test tube is fun."

"But soon, Jessica and Zee will be able to create an antidote,"

94

Diana said. She wanted to give her friends comfort and support, like any strong leader would.

"What happens if Giganta shows up again before that?" Karen asked. "I'm no Supergirl, even with her powers!"

Kara frowned. "You did an amazing job at the pumpkin patch. I'm no Bumblebee, either. You're way better in the suit than I am. Did you see how wobbly I was? It was like I'd never flown a day in my life!"

But Karen shrugged Kara's insistence and compliment off. "I just want to go back to not being very important," she said. "Some of us aren't good at being center stage." She sighed when her phone buzzed. "That's my mom. I have to go home and clean my room. Ugh."

After Karen left, Diana looked into the faces of her teammates and friends. She solemnly removed her pumpkin helmet from her head. "It breaks my warrior's spirit to think that

95

Karen Beecher does not feel like she is one of the vital hearts of this team."

"Karen is *so* important. How do we make her feel like she is?" Babs asked. Her eyes lit up. "We could beam a holograph of a bee in a heart into the night sky!"

"I will train with Karen and bond with her as true sisters in arms and justice," Diana decided. "To train alongside her is to bind us in sisterhood for eternity."

"I think Karen could use a break," Jessica said. "I'd take her on a friends' day out. We'd go to the botanical gardens, go to that new vegetarian cafe we've both been wanting to try, and maybe go to the library. Karen loves the library."

"I think the best thing I can do is figure out how to switch them back," Zee said.

"What are you thinking, Kara?" Diana asked, curious that her normally brash friend was offering no ideas.

"I'm not sure it matters what I'm thinking," Kara said. "I think it matters what I'm *feeling*. I feel unsure. It makes me wonder if Karen feels like this a lot of the time. And it makes me wonder . . . maybe it's good to feel like this sometimes. I never thought about it before. Being Supergirl means that I'm super-strong and not much can hurt me. I kind of barrel through life."

"You have confidence," Jessica said. "That's an admirable thing. But it's also something that can be hard to grow, even in the best soil."

Kara nodded in agreement.

"We all have fears," Diana said. "What matters is that we fight our fears just like we fight our foes."

"As a team!" Babs said.

"As a team," chorused the other girls, reaching out and grasping one another's hands in the kind of warrior spirit that would make the warriors of Themyscira proud.

Chapter 10

Standing Up for Yourself, Even If You're Not Completely Yourself

Now that each super hero girl had a plan to make Karen feel like a vital part of their team, they got to work making it happen.

First, Diana invited Karen to train with her. Diana was most interested in a sport that Harleen had mentioned: *gymnastics*. There were entire buildings full of things to bounce and flip off of! An acrobatic warrior's dream training ground. Karen had agreed to go to the trampoline park with Diana. It had sounded like a lot of fun. But what was supposed to be a fun training session turned into a disaster when Karen kept launching herself off the trampoline so hard she had to keep flying herself into the foam pit for safety! And more than a few times she overshot her target and smashed into the padded walls. Luckily, there were so many people bouncing and twisting in

the air that no one noticed Karen doing a little unplanned flying.

"I am sorry that our training session was not as enjoyable as I had hoped," Diana said as the two of them made their way downtown to meet Jessica for lunch.

"It was fun," Karen insisted. "All my mistakes were actually helping me get used to Kara's powers."

"Hi, you two!" Jessica waved when they arrived at the restaurant they had agreed to meet at. "How was your training session?"

MATT's VEGAN CAFE

"Karen Beecher proved herself a noble and aerodynamic warrior," Diana said.

"Super-strength and trampolines are a bad mix," Karen said. Her mouth twisted. "It's not just the powers. Having a whole new personality is no joke. I keep doing things I would never have even dreamed of before."

"Bad things?" Jessica asked as they were seated and handed menus.

Karen shook her head. "No, of course not. Kara may be a grade A rebel, but she has a heart of gold. I just keep doing things differently than I normally would. And that makes me wonder: Is Kara's way better than mine? She confronts people like Doris. I just wanted to keep quiet."

"We must all follow the beat of our own battle drum," Diana said. "Many, including my own mother, tried to keep me from competing in the Tournament of Athena and Aphrodite. But I had to follow what my heart was saying

and face the Twenty-One Challenges to become the warrior I was meant to be."

"But what if what I'm meant to be is quiet and kind of shy?" Karen asked.

"Even the quietest bee possesses a mighty sting to protect the hive," Diana said. Her encouragement made Karen smile as the server came over to take their order.

The girls asked for double of everything. Food was important for growing super heroes, especially after a battle or training session. As they finished eating and paid, Jessica asked the owner all sorts of questions about how she grew her own herbs and seasonings in a garden behind the restaurant. Before they left, the owner gave her a little pot that held a basil plant. If Jessica cared for it properly, she would be able to season her vegetarian meals with it.

"It was so nice of her to give you that," Karen said.

"I can't wait to put it in a bigger pot to allow

the roots space to wiggle their toes," Jessica said.

Karen giggled at the idea of plant roots having toes and Diana joined in with her.

"What are you goody-goodies laughing about?"

Karen whirled around, her stomach twisting when she saw that it was Doris.

"We are laughing as we enjoy the day and gifts of friendship," Diana said, like she didn't see the angry look on Doris's face.

"You shouldn't be so happy, since you got all of us detention," Doris said, right to Karen. She smiled in a mean way, like she expected Karen to start apologizing any second. And maybe last week, Karen would have done that, even though it was Doris's fault.

But Karen *wasn't* sorry. Doris deserved detention! Karen had felt bad when she noticed Doris frantically reading before their science test. She hadn't studied at all—or at

least enough. But that didn't give her the right to cheat off Karen's test. Cheaters shouldn't win, but Karen had almost *let* her win. She had only wanted Kara to drop it because it was easier.

But sometimes the easy thing wasn't the right thing. Sometimes the right thing was really hard. Sometimes it was scary. That was when doing the right thing was the most important, Karen was starting to realize.

"If you're feeling so bad about detention, maybe you should stop cheating off people's tests."

"Mr. Kincaid didn't put me in detention for cheating," Doris insisted.

Karen shot her a totally unimpressed look. She even gave her head a little defiant roll. It was a gesture she'd seen Kara make dozens of times—especially when she was getting ready for a fight. "Next time you try to cheat off me, I won't need my friend to stand up for me. I'll

tell the teacher myself."

Doris rolled her eyes and stalked away.

"Well done, Karen." Diana clapped her on the back. "You are right, you have no need for Kara to stand up for you. You do it very well on your own."

Karen smiled. She had stood up for herself, hadn't she? "I guess I have more of Kara's personality in me right now than I thought."

Diana clasped both of Karen's shoulders, looking down at her seriously. "No, Karen Beecher," she said. "That was all *you.*"

Karen wanted to believe her. She wanted to be that cool and strong. But she wondered if she only knew how to be bold when she had Supergirl's personality and powers. She and Kara were so different. She was learning that more and more every day. But she was also learning that it wasn't a bad thing. Their differences made them stronger. As girls, as heroes, and as teammates.

Chapter 11

The Quiet Before
the Storm . . . er,
Attack . . . er—Detention!

The next day, when Kara got to school, Zee excitedly pulled her into the locker room. Karen and Jessica were waiting for her there.

"Jessica and I solved it!" Zee declared, pulling a vial of blue liquid from her jacket with a flourish. "This is the antidote."

"How does it work?" Karen and Kara asked in unison.

"We apply it to your heads, and Zee does her thing," Jessica explained, making a wand-waving motion with her hand.

Karen looked at Kara, who gave her a shrug. "We gotta try something."

She was right. Jessica took the vial from Zee and tipped the liquid onto Kara's head, then Karen's. Zee took out her wand and waved it. "Hctiws pu!"

For just a moment, the air felt electric. Karen let out a surprised squeak, and Kara could sense the difference in herself instantly. She clenched her fist, feeling the power rush through her veins. Karen opened her eyes and smiled slowly as Kara sprang joyfully into the air, floating a few inches off the ground before she settled back down.

"How do you both feel?" Jessica asked.

"Back to normal," Karen said, her shoulders slumping a little. She didn't know how to feel about that. Being as bold as Kara had had its moments.

"I feel like myself again," Kara said, smoothing back her choppy hair with her hand. "In fact, I think I'll be doing some moshing tonight." She shot Karen a sly look. "Want to join me, Karen?"

Karen shook her head as the bell rang. "We're going to be late for class! Hurry!"

All the girls laughed—Kara the loudest—and followed Karen to their first class.

By the time detention rolled around at the end of the day, Kara was strutting around school like she always had. Karen had spent lunch reorganizing her locker because it had become a mess in the few days she had had Kara's personality! She was ready and eager to clean up the lab, even if it meant facing Doris without the extra boost of Kara attitude.

The lab was in disarray again. The freshman biology class was studying fungus this week. There were bits of mushroom, lichen, and all sorts of moldy-smelling things on the floor.

Karen shuddered as her foot went *squish* on something as she stepped farther into the dirty lab. Diana handed out brooms while Babs scrubbed the marble tabletops.

Jessica crouched down to collect all the mushrooms from the floor. "Did you know that fungus is its own biological kingdom of organisms?"

"Does that mean there's a Queen Mushroom?" Kara joked.

"I want to be Mushroom Queen!" Zee declared. "Imagine the outfits! Mushrooms are also excellent for spells, like pumpkins."

"No more mixing plants and spells!" Karen scolded. But she smiled at Zee to show her she wasn't actually mad.

"Hey, where's Doris?" Kara asked suddenly.

The girls looked around. They had assumed Doris was just late, but it was nearly fifteen minutes into detention. That wasn't just late.

"Did she skip detention?" Karen asked, scandalized. "Mr. Kincaid is going to be so angry!"

"It's nothing for us to worry about," Kara assured her. "It's her choice. Let's get back to work."

The girls returned to their jobs. Babs finished cleaning the lab tables, while Kara and Diana swept the floor free of fungus. Karen brought

all the lab equipment to the sink to wash. Jessica set the mushrooms she collected to the side and began to prepare a mop bucket. The girls tackled the detention assignment with the same teamwork they  used as super heroes. Soon the lab was so clean no one would ever believe that freshman biology had even had class that day.

"We did it!" Karen cheered.

But just as the girls began to put the finishing touches on the lab, a shadow fell across the room. *Crash!* A huge pumpkin came soaring through the window and splattered all over the just-cleaned lab tables and floor!

"We're under attack!" Babs shrieked.

Diana charged toward the window, fearless in the face of flying pumpkins. "It's Giganta and Harley Quinn," she said.

Kara hurried to Diana's side and peered out the smashed window. Harley Quinn was standing behind a crossbow-like machine, while Giganta was looming over a giant pile of pumpkins.

"They've got a pumpkin launcher!" Kara shouted. "And a whole lot of squash to squash!"

Chapter 12

Now Things Get Really Weird

As pumpkins went flying through the air and into the lab, the super hero girls dashed across the hallway and into the janitor's closet to transform. The commotion was sure to cause a scene, even though school was out for the day.

Wonder Woman charged forward with her Lasso of Truth swinging from her hand. Supergirl was at her side, soaring through the air with a determined expression on her face. Bumblebee followed with Green Lantern and Zatanna, while Batgirl brought up the rear, Batarangs at the ready.

Pumpkins had smashed the lab. There were pumpkin guts on the floor. On the walls. All over Mr. Kincaid's desk! He was going to be so mad!

Giganta clambered through the broken window, kicking microscopes off the back tables and knocking chairs to the ground. She was the size of a grizzly bear and equally ferocious. Behind her, Harley Quinn set her pumpkin launcher on automatic and gleefully skipped after the other villain.

"I'm gonna cover ya in pumpkin," Harley called. "You'll be so sticky you won't be able to stand it!"

"You've made the biggest mess!" Bumblebee shouted, outraged at how the lab was being treated. It was one thing for the freshman biology class to mess it up—at least they were learning! But Giganta and Harley Quinn were just causing mayhem for the sake of doing it!

"That's right, I have!" Giganta crowed. "Because I am the biggest and baddest around!"

"Do you know how long it takes to clean stuff? Because I've become an expert lately!" Supergirl shouted. She charged through the air toward Giganta, but the big bruiser batted her away. Supergirl slammed against the lab wall. She winced as she felt the walls shake. She was still getting used to having her powers back.

Wonder Woman let out a fearsome warrior

yell and leaped forward, her Lasso of Truth in hand. But she froze when Harley laughed and pulled a big beaker from behind her back.

"It's the pink foam mixed with the pumpkin!" Zatanna said, grabbing Bumblebee's arm in alarm.

"I like to go dumpster diving on the weekends," Harley cackled. "Science class always has the stickiest, stinkiest trash. And this looked really sticky. And really stinky. *And it's all for you!*"

The super hero girls were stuck! Who knew what would happen if Harley spilled the bottle on herself or Giganta? She could switch personalities with the shark in the tank, for all they knew! A Giganta shark would be scary—and scarier than a Harley shark by only a small degree.

Bumblebee noticed that Giganta's focus was on Wonder Woman and Supergirl: the people she thought were the strongest. But

Bumblebee was strong in her own way. She launched in the air, happy to be back in her suit. She zipped down to bee size, soaring forward with a determination and boldness that was *all* her.

Bumblebee grabbed the bottle out of Harley's hand and buzzed away before the clown girl even realized it was gone. Sometimes it paid to be the small, quiet one!

Bumblebee tossed the beaker to Zatanna. But before the magician could reach out and grab it, Giganta drew her arm back, planning to deliver a crushing blow. The glass container shattered on the giant's massive hand! Pink foam with pumpkin bits splattered all over Giganta and Harley.

Zatanna gasped. She had reason for the drama! The super hero girls were about to witness a villain switch-up!

Giganta shuddered as the pink foam hit her. Harley squealed.

Everyone in the room fell silent, waiting to see what would happen. Were the villains going to switch powers and personalities like Kara and Karen had? Or would the strange mix of science, squash, and magic cause a different reaction in them?

The super hero girls got the answer to their questions almost instantly. A poster fell off the wall, brushing against Giganta's shoulder. Instead of batting it away angrily, Giganta giggled like it tickled! Giganta wasn't ticklish!

The super hero girls watched as Harley Quinn looked down at her fingernails and gasped. "I don't paint my nails red and blue!" Harley said in a much deeper voice than her normal squeak. Then she gave a sinister chuckle.

Giganta stared at herself in the broken window's reflection and began to hum, arranging her hair into pigtails. Harley muttered under her breath and pulled her pigtails out, brushing through her hair angrily until it was wild around her face.

"It's a full-body switcheroo this time!" Zatanna shouted in realization. "Giganta is in Harley's body, and Harley is in Giganta's body!"

"Jeepers!" Harley-as-Giganta said. "This is somethin' else!"

"Just remain calm," Wonder Woman told the villains. "Do you have any ideas?" she asked Zatanna under her breath.

Giganta-as-Harley began to pace and stomp. "Why won't I grow?" she growled. "And why are my arms so puny?!"

"I see why you like being so big!" Harley-as-Giganta giggled, bouncing up and down in excitement. "I'm so strong!" She flexed her biceps. "Ooo . . . muscles!"

"Those are *my* muscles!" Giganta-as-Harley roared in anger. "You didn't put in the work to earn them!"

"Harley, you need to stay still," Zatanna said. "You only got sprayed with a little foam. It should wear off in a few minutes."

"I don't think so!" Harley-as-Giganta said. "I wanna try my new powers out. I think it's time for some acrobatics!" Before anyone could stop her, she began to flip and cartwheel across the lab, smashing tables and chairs in her destructive enthusiasm. This time, her routine didn't just make the lab floor shake, it sent the team flying—even the ones who

127

couldn't fly! Luckily, they got to their feet in seconds. Harley-as-Giganta was dangerous! She wasn't going to be patient and figure out how Giganta's powers worked. She was just going to smash everything and giggle about it.

Giganta-as-Harley did some quick thinking while the super heroes were distracted by Harley's antics. She didn't have her powers, and Harley's body was terrible at crushing things. *Tee-hee!* That was it! She needed to *think* like Harley instead. Giganta-as-Harley leaped out the window, grabbed Harley's pumpkin launcher, and loaded up six pumpkins at once.

"Time to get squashed, Super Hero Girls!" she yelled, pressing the big orange button.

Bumblebee yanked Supergirl out of the way as one of the pumpkins crashed to the floor right where she had been standing. Another pumpkin smashed into the fish tank. Wonder Woman gasped in horror as the shark went flying through the air.

"Baby!" Harley-as-Giganta held out her arms and caught the shark! She hugged the sea creature to her and some of the magic pink foam on her face smeared onto the shark. *Pop!*

Harley-as-Giganta let out a startled shriek as the shark began to grow and grow. She dropped it with a yelp as she began to shrink.

Behind the pumpkin launcher, Giganta-as-Harley watched as Harley-as-Giganta got smaller and the shark grew. They needed to get out of here before Harley lost her giant powers completely! "Harley!" she shouted. "It's time to scram!"

Realizing that this was their chance to get away, Harley-as-Giganta dashed through

the broken windows and joined Giganta-as-Harley while the super hero girls rushed to the shark's aid.

Harley-as-Giganta was getting smaller with each step she took, but the super hero girls knew they couldn't chase the villains down *and* save Kerfuffle.

Green Lantern used her power ring to create a net to keep the shark from flopping all over the floor while Zatanna cast a spell to repair the fish tank—"Erotser ssalg!" Bumblebee and Wonder Woman hurried back and forth between the tank and the sink, filling it with water.

Zatanna tossed the test tube with the remaining antidote into the air. "On it!" Bumblebee shouted, as she landed on the top of the test tube, her weight tipping it, and emptying the last of the blue liquid into the water.

Zatanna waved her wand and said "Retawaes!" to make the water go from fresh water to salt water. Then Green Lantern transformed the green net into a sliding board and carefully slid the shark into the tank. Kerfuffle splashed about as if nothing had happened.

Wonder Woman pressed a hand to her heart, her eyes shining like a thousand suns. "A warrior could not hope for better sisters," she said. "You have saved Kerfuffle!"

"Did she actually *name* the shark Kerfuffle?" Supergirl asked Bumblebee.

"It kind of fits," Bumblebee pointed out. She glanced at the clock on the wall and let out

a shriek. "Girls! We have ten minutes before Mr. Kincaid comes to check on the lab!"

With Kerfuffle safely back in her tank, the super hero girls went to work on the lab, this time using their superpowers! As Zatanna fixed the broken windows with magic, Bumblebee turned off Harley Quinn's pumpkin launcher and stowed it out of sight. Wonder Woman and Batgirl carefully filled bags full of smashed pumpkin parts, and Supergirl sped them away to the dumpster. A lot of hard work, speed,

and a bit of magic got the job done. When Mr. Kincaid walked into the room, the lab was spotless.

The teacher frowned when he saw the girls—now in their normal clothes—lined up at the front of the room, waiting for him. "Done already?"

"We wanted to make up for last time," Karen explained.

"We felt bad about what a mess it was," Kara added. She thought that she might even keep her own room clean from now on. Well, *cleaner,* at least.

"I'm glad you learned from this," Mr. Kincaid said. "And since you have done such a good job, I will share the exciting news I've just received. Metropolis High has caught the eye of the very prestigious Project Cadmus."

"The science company?" Babs asked, her eyes going wide with excitement.

"They're considering coming to our school to be judges in the upcoming science fair. There might even be an internship for the winning student and a grant for the winning school."

Karen, Babs, and Jessica squealed in excitement. This was the best news for

science-minded students at Metropolis High ever! Thank goodness they had gotten the lab clean—and Kara and Karen had gotten switched back to their old selves. Mr. Kincaid would never have let Project Cadmus come to the lab if he'd seen Giganta and Harley Quinn's path of destruction. No scientist worth their lab goggles would've worked in such a mess!

This time, when the girls assembled, it was for an excited hug. An upcoming science fair, *and* a possible internship and grant for the school? The life of the curious student by day and super hero at night could not get better!

Chapter 13

One . . . Two . . . Three . . . Frosting Smash!

After detention, the super hero girls went to Sweet Justice, their favorite treats shop. They deserved some cupcakes.

"I never thought I'd say it, but I think I learned more from detention than school in the last few days," Kara said as they sat at their regular table.

Babs giggled.

"I learned not to mix magic, squash, and science," Zee said. "Never again!"

Diana swiped a finger through the frosting on her cookies-and-cream cupcake. "I learned

about unicorns, the word 'kerfuffle,' and that faithful friends are forever."

"Oh, I like that last one," Babs said cheerfully. "I also learned that faithful friends are forever."

"I learned that the need to protect pumpkins and squash is clearly growing," Jessica said. "While I don't think I can convince people to stop buying them just to carve, I could create a program to compost pumpkins."

"That's a great idea," Karen said. "I want to help."

"As will I," Diana said. "And what do you think, Kara Danvers?" she asked. "What have you learned from detention and this switcheroo that has bonded you and Karen as sisters in both power and heart?"

Kara grinned. "You know, I think the coolest thing I learned was that Karen is a little more rock and roll than I thought. The girl knows how to mosh." She winked at her friend.

Karen blushed at the compliment. "And I would say that Kara is a lot more patient than any of us give her credit for," she said. "She may be a hothead"—Kara laughed and nodded—"but she holds back a lot so that she can give it her all when she's needed most."

"Did you like having a hot head?" Kara asked.

138

"It was a lot of fun, feeling like the world couldn't touch me," Karen admitted. "Being confident can be hard. Even though I'm not indestructible, I'm going to try to keep feeling that way. Because I deserve to."

"Yes you do!" her friends cheered.

"We also learned that cheaters never prosper!" Babs said excitedly. "I heard that Mr. Kincaid gave Doris another full week's worth of detention for not showing up to clean the lab with us!"

"In time, perhaps she will learn the lessons we have learned," Diana said.

"I'm not sure there are enough test tubes in the world to scrub to teach her," Kara said, "but I wish Mr. Kincaid luck!"

"Let's do a cupcake toast," Karen said. She held out her red velvet cupcake. "To being brave and doing the right thing, even when it's scary!"

The girls tapped their cupcakes together.

The frosting didn't clink, but it did smash, and it was a good kind of mess this time.

A very good kind of mess indeed.